PERCY AND THE FIVE HOUSES

by **Else Holmelund Minarik**

pictures by **James Stevenson**

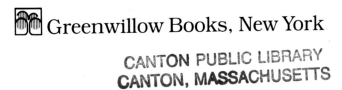 Greenwillow Books, New York

Watercolor paints and a black pen
were used for the full-color art.
The text type is ITC Bookman.

Library of Congress Cataloging-in-Publication Data
Minarik, Else Holmelund.
Percy and the five houses.
Summary: None of the five different houses
Percy receives from the House of the Month Club
proves to be as perfect as his own beaver home.
[1. Dwellings—Fiction.   2. Beavers—Fiction]
I. Stevenson, James (date)   ill.   II. Title.
PZ7.M652Pe 1989   [E]   88-4804
ISBN 0-688-08104-5
ISBN 0-688-08105-3 (lib. bdg.)

FOR BOB AND KAS BENDINER,

FOUNDERS

OF THE

HOUSE

OF THE

MONTH

CLUB

It was a fine day in July.

Percy played by the river.

There he found some gold.

"Why—that's real gold!" said Grandpa.

Lucky Percy.

He was rich!

Along came Ferd the fox.

"I am rich," said Percy to Ferd.

"See my gold."

"My, my!" said Ferd. "So you are,
Percy. Now you can belong to
The House of the Month Club."

"If you give me the gold," said Ferd,

"I can put your name on this card,

like this:

HOUSE OF THE MONTH
CLUB

PERCY

Then you will belong to the club."

"What is The House of the Month Club?"
Percy wanted to know.
"The House of the Month Club is a club
that sends you a house a month,"
said Ferd. "You will have
an August house, a September house,
an October house, a November house,
and a December house."

"I like that," said Percy.

"Here is the gold, Ferd."

"And here is your card, Percy,"
said Ferd. "Now you belong to the
club. You are a lucky beaver!"

In August the first house came.

It came in a big box.

It was a cardboard house.

Grandpa and Percy took it out

and put it all together.

What a fancy house!

Percy ran to call the family.

They all came to see the new house.

There it was, up in a tree.

"The wind took it," said Grandpa.

That was too bad.

But the birds liked it.

In September a second house came.
Grandpa and Percy put it together.
It was a castle—
a real cardboard castle!
Percy and his friends played in it
—and on it
—and all through it.

And then it rained.

Soon there was no more castle.

"I can't wait for October,"

said Percy.

In October a third house came.

It came in a small package.

What could be in that small package?

Why—it was a teepee!

It was a beautiful Indian teepee,

all made of crepe paper.

Now wasn't that fun!

Too bad, the fun did not last long.

Soon the teepee was gone.

Everyone had a little bit of it.

What would come in November?

Percy could not wait for November.

In November another small package came.

And in it was a dear little camper.

Grandpa put the wheels on it.

"But it is too small!" said Percy.

"Not for us," said some mice.

They pulled it away.

And that was that.

"What next?" said Grandpa to Percy.

It was growing cold.
It was icy and snowy.
And then in December a truck
pulled up. Ferd got out and
unloaded the truck.

"Look here, Percy," he said.

"This is your last house.

 How do you like it?"

"An igloo!" cried Percy.

"My goodness!" said Grandpa.

"We don't need it!" said Mother.
"We don't need one more house!
 We have one, you know, out there
 in the water.
 It won't blow away.
 It won't fall down.
 It won't tear,
 and we can all fit into it.
 So come along, you two. Winter is here,
 and everyone is waiting for you."

"Well, Ferd," said Percy.

"You can have the igloo."

"Why—thank you," said Ferd.

"I will vacation at the North Pole."

Percy and Ferd loaded the igloo

back into the truck.

"I'm off," said Ferd.

He waved to Percy.

Percy waved back.

Soon Ferd was out of sight.

Percy slid down into the water.

He swam out slowly.

He made a wide circle.

He ducked under.

Then he was home.

"I know something," said Percy to the family.

"I know that this little house is the best
house for beavers."

"Percy," said Grandpa, "you are absolutely right!
This is the best little house for us!"

E   c.1

5/89

Minarik.

Percy and the five houses.